FORT WORTH PUBLIC LIBRARY

W9-BNU-826

CHILDREN 428.1 NICKLE 2006
Nickle, John
Alphabet explosion!

Bold

BOLD BRANCH

To John and Sara

Copyright © 2006 by John Nickle

All rights reserved.
Published in the United States by Schwartz & Wade Books, an imprint of Random
House Children's Books, a division of Random House, Inc., New York.

SCHWARTZ & WADE BOOKS and colophon are trademarks of Random House, Inc.

www.randomhouse.com/kids

Educators and librarians, for a variety of teaching tools, visit us at
www.randomhouse.com/teachers

Library of Congress Cataloging-in-Publication Data

Nickle, John.
Alphabet explosion! : Search and Count from Alien to Zebra /
John Nickle.— 1st ed.
p. cm.
ISBN-10: 0-375-83598-9 (tr.) 0-375-93598-3 (lib. bdg.)
ISBN-13: 978-0-375-83598-8 (tr.) 978-0-375-93598-5 (lib. bdg.)
1. English language—Alphabet—Juvenile literature.
I. Title.

PE1155.N534 2006
428.1'3—dc22
2005024372

The text of this book is set in Franklin Gothic, Fairfield, and Helvetica Neue.
The illustrations are rendered in acrylic and spray paint on watercolor paper.

Book design by Rachael Cole

MANUFACTURED IN CHINA

10 9 8 7 6 5 4 3 2 1

First Edition

ALPHABET EXPLOSION !

SEARCH AND COUNT FROM ALIEN TO ZEBRA BY JOHN NICKLE

FORT WORTH PUBLIC LIBRARY

schwartz & wade books · new york

HOW TO PLAY

SEE HOW MANY YOU CAN FIND!

In each picture there are a certain number of things that begin with the same letter. Our team of alphabet experts has searched, and we think we have found them all. Our answers are on the bottom of each page, with the specific items we found listed at the back of the book.

WHAT TO COUNT:

Objects, actions, and colors should all be counted. For example, on the R page, "rain" and "raining" count as two R's. "Red" also counts.

If the number of objects begins with the same letter as the object itself, then count that number. For example, "four fish" counts as two F's.

An object that is made up of two words beginning with the same letter counts twice. For example, "bowling ball" counts as two B's. (However, "yo-yo" is only one word and counts as one Y.)

Don't forget to count the upper- and lowercase letters that appear on each page!

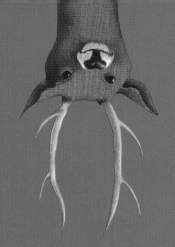

WHAT NOT TO COUNT:

Don't count any shapes that look like the letters. For example, on the O page, the round suction cups on the octopus should not be counted.

If you see something that appears several times, count it only once. For instance, there are many eyes on the E page. Just count them once. (However, if there are eleven eyes, count that as two E's.)

If you find more things than we did, please contact our Chief Alphabet Expert (who also happens to have created the pictures), John Nickle, at abc@johnnickle.net, and let him know.

AND IF YOU FIND FEWER, DON'T WORRY—IT'S TRICKY!

22 A's

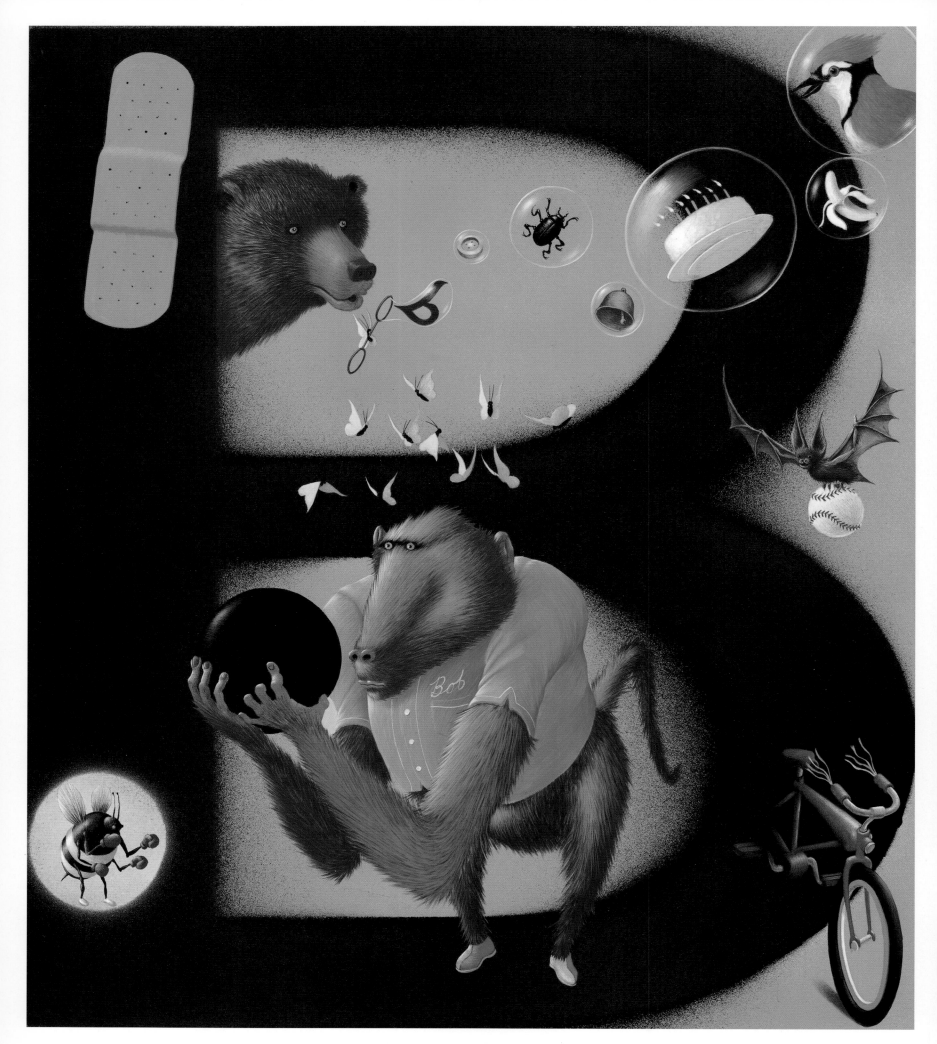

29 B's

32 C's

20 D's

21 E's

25 F's

25 G's

24 H's

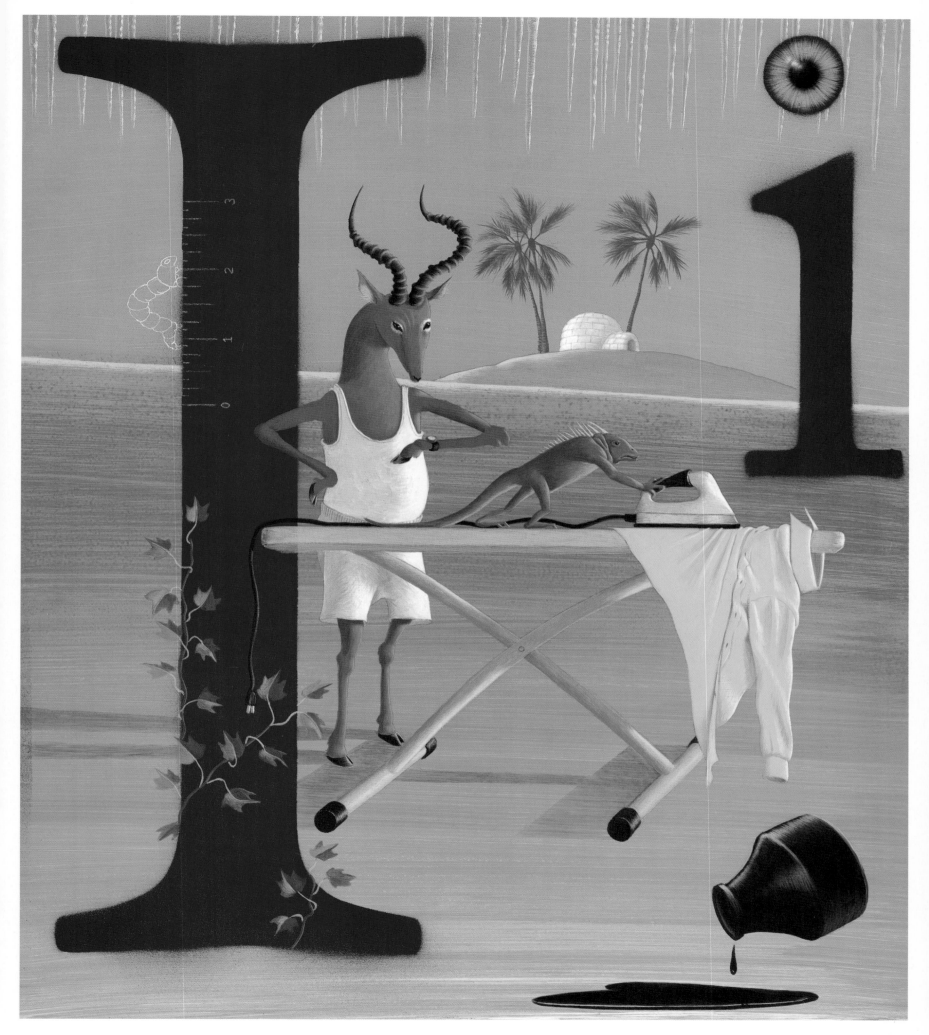

17 I's

16 J's

20 K's

26 L's

21 M's

20 N's

15 O's

32 P's

7 Q's

27 R's

47 S's

32 T's

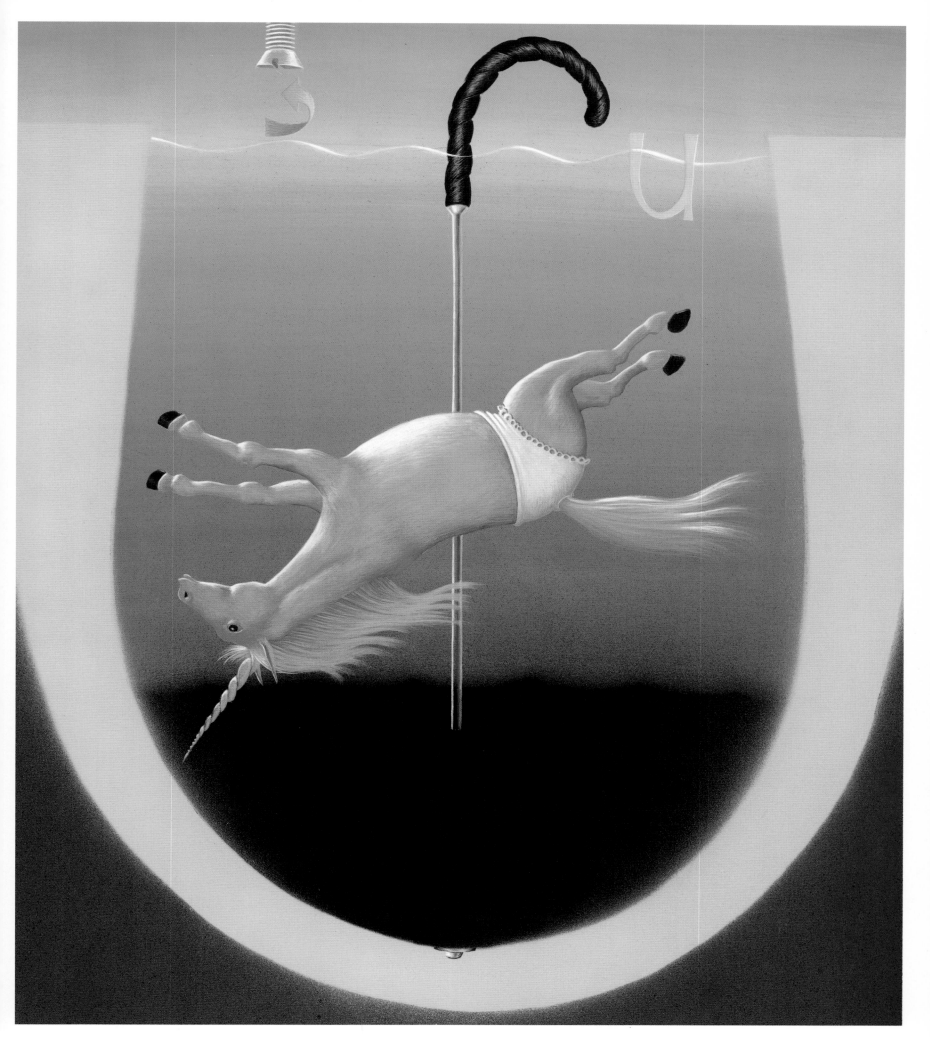

8 U's

19 V's

25 W's

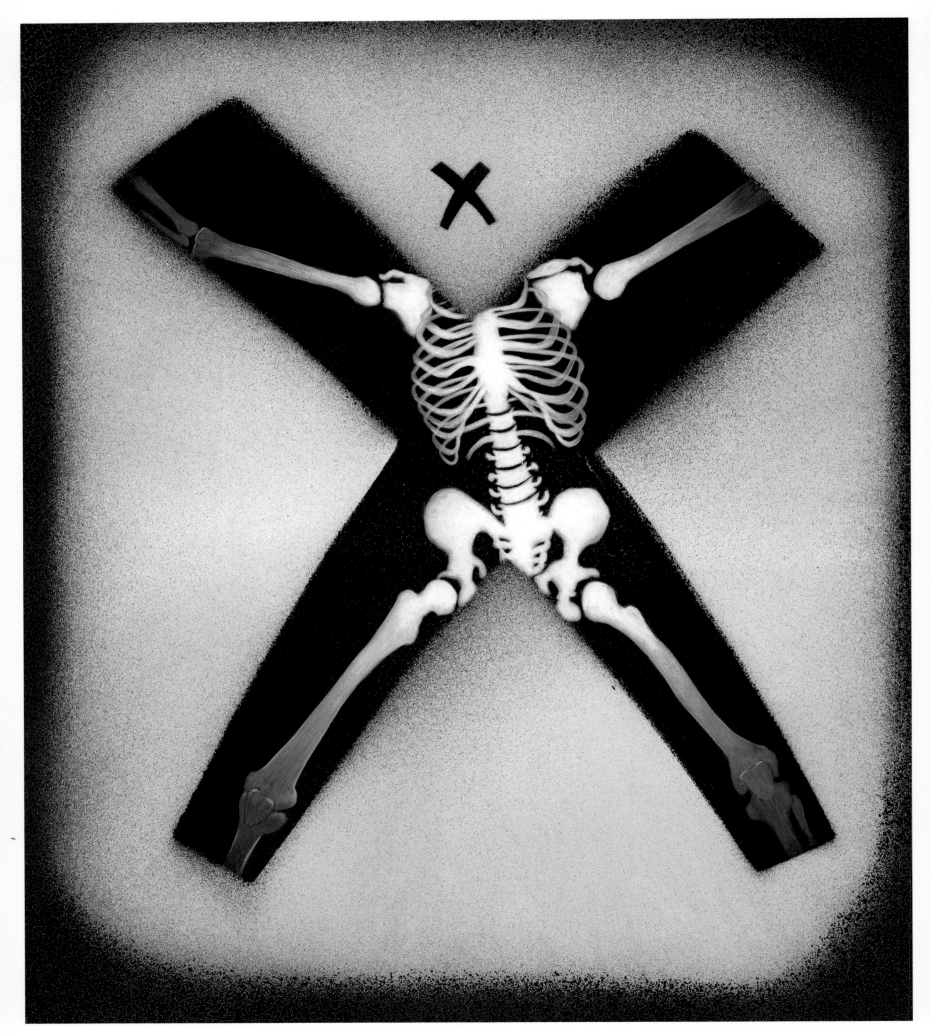

3 X's

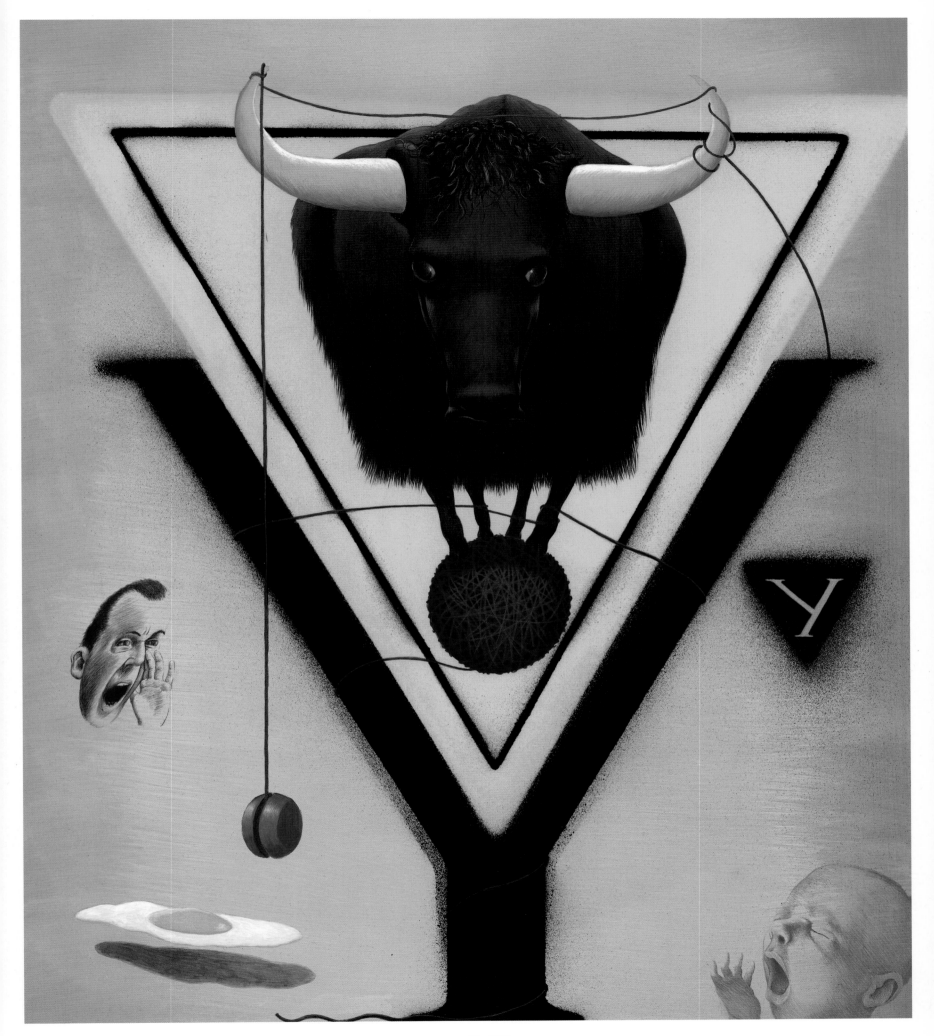

10 Y's

7 Z's

A
A, a, aardvark, accordion, acorn, Afro, aiming, airplane, alarm clock, alien, alligator, ambulance, anchor, ant, antennae, anvil, apple, apron, archer, arms, arrow, atom

B
B, b, baboon, banana, Band-Aid, baseball, bat, beak, bear, bee, beetle, bell, bicycle, birthday cake, black, blowing, blue, blue jay, Bob, bowling, bowling ball, boxing, boxing gloves, brown, bubbles, bubble wand, butterflies, button

C
C, c, camel, candle, candle holder, candy cane, cap, cape, car, cardinal, carrying, cat, caterpillar, chain, checkerboard, chickens, circle, claws, cliff, cloud, club, coffee cup, cone, convertible, corncob, corner, cow, crossing, crow, crown

D
D, d, daisy, dancing, deer, dentist, derby, diamonds, dice, dinosaur, dogs, dolphin, donkey, door, doorknob, dots, dreaming, dresses, drop, duck

E
E, e, eagle, ears, earth, earthworm, earwig, eating, egg, eight, eight ball, electric eel, electricity, elephant, elf, eraser, erasing, Eskimo, eyebrows, eyes

F
F, f, face, feathers, fence, finger, fingernail, fins, fire, fireman, fishhook, fishing, fishing rod, five flowers, flamingo, flute, fly, flying, foot, four fish, fox, frog, fur

G
G, g, galoshes, ghost, gift, giraffe, girl, giving, glass, glasses, gloves, goat, goldfish, gopher, gorilla, golf ball, golf club, golfing, goose, grass, grasshopper, green, grinning, guess who, guitar

H
H, h, hair, halo, hand, happy, hare, hat, head, hexagon, hill, hippopotamus, hive, hole, honeycomb, hopping, hopscotch, hot dog, house, hula, Hula Hoop, Humpty Dumpty, hyenas

I I, i, icicles, igloo, iguana, impala, impatient, inches, inchworm, ink, ink bottle, iris, iron, ironing, ironing board, island, ivy

J J, j, jacket, jackhammer, jackrabbit, jacks, jailbird, jelly beans, jellyfish, jester, jet, jewels, jockey, judge, juggling, jump rope

K K, k, kangaroo, kettle, khaki, kick, kilt, king, kingfisher, kiss, kite, kitten, kiwi, kneeling, knees, knee socks, knight, knitting, knitting needles, knot

L L, l, ladder, lady, ladybug, lamb, lamp, lampshade, Laundromat, laundry, lawn, lawn mower, legs, lemon, lemur, letter, librarian, library, licking, lighthouse, lion, lips, litter box, lizard, llama, lobster

M M, m, mail, mailbox, mailing, man in the moon, mermaids, milk, milk bottle, mittens, mole, monkeys, moon, moose, mosquito, moths, mouse, mouth, muscle, mushrooms

N N, n, naked, narwhal, neck, necklace, necktie, needle, needlefish, nest, net, newt, night, nighthawk, nightingale, nine nails, nose, notebook, nurse

O O, o, oar, octopus, olive, one o'clock, onion, opossum, orange, orbit, otter, oval, overalls, owl

P P, p, pajamas, paintbrush, painting, panda, pants, paper hat, parachute, parachuting, parrot, patch, paw, pea, penguin, perching, pig, pillow, pin, pink, pipe, pocket, polka dots, poodle, pool, popping, porcupine, porpoise, portrait (or picture), posing, princess, purple

Q Q, q, quail, quarter, queen, question mark, quilt

R, r, rabbit, raccoon, radish, rain, raindrops, raining, rake, rat, raven, reading, red, refrigerator, rhinoceros, riding, roach, roadrunner, robin, robot, rocket, roller skates, roller skating, rooster, roots, roses, running

S, s, saddle shoe, sailboat, sailor hat, scarf, scissors, seven stars, shadow, shark, sheep, shell, shoelace, shovel, singing, six squares, skis, skull, sledding, sleeping, slippers, slithering, snail, snake, snow, snowman, socks, song, sparrow, spider, spiral, squirrel, stairs, starfish, stepping, sticks, stop sign, stork, stripes, submarine, sun, sunflower, sunglasses (or spectacles)

T, t, tan, tapir, talking, target, taxi, teddy bear, teeth, telephone, thirteen trees, three tails, throwing, tiger, tires, toad, toenails, tomatoes, towing, tow truck, toys, trunk, turquoise, twelve (pieces of) toast, twenty toes, two turtles

U, u, umbrella, underwater, underwear, unicorn, unscrewing, upside down

V, v, vacuum, vacuuming, valentine, vampire, van, vase, veil, vest, veterinarian, Viking, violets, violin, violinist, viper, volcano, volleyball, vulture

W, w, waffle, waitress, walking, wall, walrus, wart, water, weasel, weight lifting, weights, whale, whistle, whistling, white, wig, windmill, window, wings, witch, wood, woodpecker, wolf, wrinkles

X, x, X-ray

Y, y, yak, yarn, yawn, yelling, yellow, yield sign, yolk, yo-yo

Z, z, zebra, zero, zipper, zipping, zoo